THE FATHER OF A MURDERER

Alfred Andersch

The Father
of a Murderer

Translated by Leila Vennewitz

A NEW DIRECTIONS BOOK

The Father of a Murderer is published by arrangement with Diogenes Verlag, Zurich, who originally brought out *Der Vater eines Mörders* in 1980.

Manufactured in the United States of America
New Directions Books are printed on acid-free paper.
First published clothbound in 1994
Published simultaneously in Canada by Penguin Books Canada Limited

Library of Congress Cataloging-in-Publication Data

Andersch, Alfred, 1914–
   [Vater eines Mörders. English]
   The father of a murderer / Alfred Andersch ; translated by Leila Vennewitz.
     p.   cm.
   ISBN 0–8112–1261–0 (alk. paper)
   I. Title.
PT2601.N353V3813   1994
833'.914—dc20   93–50806
                                                 CIP

New Directions Books are published for James Laughlin
by New Directions Publishing Corporation,
80 Eighth Avenue, New York 10011

An untalented *Gymnasium* student
dedicates this story
to a highly talented one,
who became one of the greatest masters
of German language and literature:
to his contemporary and dear friend
Arno Schmidt
in memoriam

TRANSLATOR'S ACKNOWLEDGMENT

My thanks are due to Bruce Clausen and Maryke Gilmore for their invaluable assistance concerning classical Greek.

I am also deeply grateful to my husband William for his unstinting contribution of special skills and knowledge.

Leila Vennewitz

Of this one, so I hear, we have been rid,
And he will not continue as before.
He has now ceased to murder us.
Sad to say, there's no more to describe,
Of this one, so you see, we have been rid.
But I know of many who are still among us.

Bertolt Brecht
"On the Death of a Criminal"

"Almost nobody seems to feel that the sin committed hourly against our children is part of the very *nature* of school. But the nations must one day suffer the consequences of having turned their schools into institutions in which the soul of the child is systematically murdered."

Fritz Mauthner
Dictionary of Philosophy

CONTENTS

THE FATHER OF A MURDERER

The Greek lesson was about to begin when the door to the classroom opened once again. Franz Kien did not pay much attention to the opening of the door. It was only when he noticed their homeroom teacher, Mr. Kandlbinder, stand up with a look of annoyance or even alarm, turn toward the door, and come down the two steps from his desk—something he would never have done if the person entering had been merely a student—only then did Franz Kien look with curiosity toward the door, which was at the front on the right, next to the dais on which the blackboard stood. He saw at once that it was the Headmaster entering the classroom: he was wearing a light-weight, pale-gray suit, the jacket unbuttoned, and under the jacket a white shirt bulged over his paunch. For a moment the stout figure stood out palely against the gray corridor outside. Then the door closed behind him. Someone who had accompanied him but remained invisible must have opened and closed it again: the door had moved on its hinges like an automat releasing a doll. Just the way those figures pop out from the city hall tower on Marien-Platz, thought Franz Kien.

In his discomfiture Mr. Kandlbinder—still with an expression as if he were murmuring to himself, "God give me strength!"—called out a second too late: "All rise!" But the boys had already risen without waiting for his order. Nor did they wait to sit down until their teacher managed—again a split second too late—to bring out the words: "Sit down!" They had already done so when the Head, raising his hands in protest, told the young teacher: "Please tell them to sit down!"

From their double benches, which formed a solid unit with the double desks—the boys had to squeeze between bench and desk, most of them at fourteen having already outgrown them—they observed Kandlbinder's confusion and how skillfully the Head thwarted the young teacher's attempt at a bow by shaking his hand. Although Kandlbinder was some five inches taller than the Head, who wasn't exactly short—about five foot nine, Franz Kien guessed—suddenly they could all see that their teacher, standing like that beside the corpulent and obviously robust Headmaster, was merely a skinny, pale-faced, insignificant person, and for a second it flashed upon them why they knew nothing about him except that he also knew nothing about them, and that in a level monotone he gave lessons which were no doubt great stuff, except that, especially toward the end of a period, they found it hard to stay awake. Holy cow, what a bore this Kandlbinder is! Franz had sometimes thought. Yet he's still quite young! A colorless complexion, but his black hair always a bit untidy.

For a while Franz and his classmates had watched expectantly to see whether Kandlbinder, who took over their Grade 8 class after Easter at the start of the school year, would pick a favorite, or maybe a boy he obviously couldn't stand. But meanwhile almost two months had gone by, and so far the teacher had carefully avoided any indication of that kind. The only time he had gone off the rails, Franz thought, was during that row with Konrad Greiff. During recess or on their way to and from school, when they discussed Kandlbinder's reserve—which, since the teacher held little interest for them, didn't happen very often— there would always be someone who would remark with a shrug: "He just wants to keep his distance."

The Head had turned toward the class. Behind the gold-rimmed spectacles the blue eyes were sharply observant. The gold and blue combined to form something sparkling, lively, a look of kindliness and benevolence showing now in a rosy face beneath smooth white hair. But Franz immediately sensed that the Head, although capable of assuming a benign appearance, was not entirely harmless; his affability was certainly not to be trusted, not even now when, jovial and portly, he gazed at the boys seated in three double rows in front of him.

"Well, well," he said, "so this is my Grade 8-B! I am happy to see you!"

He really is a Head, thought Franz, not just a head-master whose title had been abbreviated in the Wittelsbach *Gymnasium*. The headmasters of other Munich schools were also called "Head," yet Franz doubted whether most of them looked authoritative. But this one did. Pale-gray and white—over the shirt lay, immaculately, a shiny blue tie—on his face that gold and blue, rounded visor—he stood against the background of the big blackboard, and neither Kandlbinder nor the students seemed to be offended by his imposing the possessive pronoun on the class. Am I the only one, Franz wondered, who has noticed that he addressed us as if he owned us? He made up his mind to ask Hugo Aletter, when the class was over, whether he didn't find it presumptuous of the Head, merely because he was Headmaster, to feel justified in describing the class as his property.

Hugo Aletter, with whom he shared a desk, wasn't his best friend in the class—Franz had no close friend among his classmates—but he was the only one to whom he dared put such a question. He could even discuss politics with Hugo; sometimes they did this during recess in a corner of the school playground, using terms picked up from listening to the talk of their nationalistic fathers. And it was for this reason, not out of friendship, that they had chosen to sit together in class. The others had also been hearing at home the phrases making up the political discussions of the Munich middle class, but they ignored them; these "kids," as Franz and Hugo contemptuously called them, were not interested in politics. But maybe not even Hugo would understand, thought Franz, what it is that bothers me about the Head addressing us as "my Grade 8-B." I'm not sure myself, and it certainly has nothing to do with politics. Suddenly he remembered his father, who had been an officer in the 1914–18 war, although only in the Reserves. He, too, always talked about "my men" when he dug up his wartime memories, and it never occurred to me, thought Franz, that such a phrase could be any less natural than my thinking of my father as "my father."

"Greek!" said the Head. "I hope it is not going to cause you as much trouble as it does 8-A!" He shook his head. "What a performance! Tsk, tsk, tsk!"

This conveyed to them that he had already inspected their parallel class. It must have just happened, for it was now eleven o'clock, and if he had shown up in A the previous day, or even before recess that morning, the boys in B would have heard about it from their friends in A, with the necessary warnings: "Be prepared for the Head!" So it was clear that the Headmaster had intended to take the classes by surprise. Obviously he had been careful to avoid giving any hint of this to his teaching staff, for even Kandlbinder had had no inkling of the impromptu visit, or he wouldn't have been so aghast when the Headmaster appeared.

The latter had succeeded, especially by the tongue-clicking that followed his remark, in creating the impression among his listeners that he considered them capable of sharing his concern over the deplorable performance of their parallel class. He was grieved, and he let them share this feeling; he took it for granted that the B class agreed that it was disgraceful, indeed incomprehensible, to fail in Greek: it was a case, not of a serious though curable disease, but of a blemish, incomprehensible, calling for a disgruntled, impatient tsk-tsk-tsk, as if this summed it all up. At least that was how it seemed to Franz, without, however, his inferring from this impression—somewhat vague though it was—that the Head might be a poor schoolmaster. On the contrary, he was also taken in by the tsk-tsk-tsk trick, felt flattered by the confidence the Head seemed to place in them, and resolved to try to do better in Greek in the future.

He didn't bother to ascertain how Kandlbinder reacted to the two sentences with which the Head announced that he had already weighed the boys in A class and found them wanting. Did Kandlbinder regard those words as a threat, as a warning of what lay in store for him, the teacher, should his class likewise fail to measure up? Or did he interpret them as an opportunity because in view of his ponderous but exemplary teaching, the excellent results of which were beyond doubt, he felt that nothing could possibly go wrong? Franz thought no more about it; this dry-as-dust pedant, whose Greek classes he had so far managed successfully to cheat his way through, simply didn't interest him enough to claim his attention, for then he would have missed watching the Head who, in contrast to Kandlbinder, was putting on such an exciting, although dangerously exciting, show.

"Don't let me disturb you, Dr. Kandlbinder!" the Head now said. "Just carry on!"

Carry on, that's a joke, thought Franz indignantly. The Head had come in literally during the first minute of the lesson; it was downright unfair to act as if Kandlbinder had been able even to get started. On the other hand, the Head immediately managed to enhance the teacher's reputation in the eyes of the students by conveying the fact that he was a Ph.D. This was news to the class. *Dr.* Kandlbinder. It might not seem anything special in a school where it was customary for all the teachers, from the most junior to the most senior, to be addressed as "Professor." However, it did confer a distinction on their teacher, for this much they already knew about academic titles and ranks: that a teacher with a Ph.D. ranks higher than one who, although addressed as "Professor," has not written a doctoral thesis, not earned a doctorate.

"Of course, Headmaster," said Kandlbinder and called upon Werner Schröter. "Schröter," he said, "would you mind coming up to the front?"

So that's how they address each other, thought Franz. Doctor, Headmaster. To us they say *Du*—only in Grade 9 do they switch to *Sie*. If I have to repeat eighth grade—and most likely I will—because of failing Greek and math, and failing two major subjects always means repeating the grade, they'll go on saying *Du* to me for another year. I don't care. What's the difference? There are more important things. What would have been more important to him, Franz Kien couldn't have said.

"Schröter," said Kandlbinder, "since we are now doing phonetics, I would like you to write the double consonants on the board."

Kandlbinder's lost his marbles, thought Franz, he hasn't come to yet, the Head's arrival to check up on his class has thrown him for a loop. What absolute madness to waste his best ammunition right at the

start instead of saving it up in case something goes
wrong! Or producing him later as a star turn. And then
to set him such a dead-easy task! Even I could write
the three double consonants! We learned those ages
ago—we're already tackling euphonic changes and
have even gone beyond that in the grammar, as far as
word-formation rules. Kandlbinder had quite a way of
jumping back and forth in the grammar. Franz
smirked: If their teacher only knew that the Greek
grammar he, Franz, had absorbed amounted to little
more than the heading of each chapter they were
studying! When it came to homework he got help from
his brother Karl, who had inexplicably progressed to
Grade 10, although he was as great a washout as Franz
in the main subjects, especially languages. How on
earth had he managed to get as far as Grade 10? By
taking such ridiculous pains, Franz supposed: pulling
the wool over his teachers' eyes with his small, neat,
regular handwriting that covers sheet after sheet; his
homework is full of mistakes, just like mine, but the
writing always looks like copperplate. I can't be
bothered—couldn't do it if I tried. Franz wrote in a
scrawl, sometimes sloppy, sometimes jagged; the
teachers shook their heads as they looked at his homework. Professor Burckhardt, the biology teacher, who
liked Franz, although the boy was no good in this
subject either, would say from time to time: "Kien,

why don't you try to give some form to your handwriting?" He of all people, Franz always thought, since Burckhardt himself had trouble drawing the outline of a blossom—of the cuckoo-flower, say—on the blackboard. The chalk kept breaking off, and eventually he would fling it down and exclaim: "Look it up in your textbook—it's in there!"

After Schröter had been called to the board, the Head sat down at the teacher's desk, where they could all see him picking up the open Greek grammar lying there and immersing himself in it. Or was he merely pretending to be absorbed in the subject at hand? In any case, he seemed to show as little interest in the boy at the blackboard as the boy did in him. Typical of Schröter, thought Franz, as he watched him set out unhurriedly to clean one corner of the blackboard, it being quite unthinkable for him to use a surface that the blackboard monitor had merely wiped with a dry sponge or cloth so that it was covered with gray smears instead of looking, as a blackboard should, like black shoe polish. So Schröter, while ignoring the presence of the school's supreme ruler—of the Grand Panjandrum, thought Franz, but of course Schröter can afford to do this—walked casually over to the faucet near the blackboard, wetted the sponge, squeezed it half dry, and proceeded to transform the upper corner of the blackboard into a shiny black surface, which he then dried with the cloth before writing the ξ, the ψ, and the ζ, pronouncing the letters one by one as if talking to himself, or at least without being asked to by Kandlbinder: "Ksi, psi, dsi."

In contrast to the Head, who was still busy studying the grammar, Kandlbinder, painfully embarrassed and constantly glancing at his superior enthroned behind his own desk, waited until Schröter had finished. Now at last he took the plunge: "Although it is customary to pronounce an i," he said, "actually it is incorrect. These are pure double consonants. So: ks, ps, ds." So excellent was his rendering of the palatal, labial, and dental sounds, especially of the labial initial sound of the psi, that Franz resolved to refer to him among the others after class as "Kandl-p-inder." He never dreamed that after this class he would no longer be in the mood for jokes of any kind.

"Come, come, Dr. Kandlbinder," said the Head, looking up from the grammar, and with these two monosyllables revoking his recently granted, generous permission for Kandlbinder to carry on. "We are not altogether certain, are we, how the ancient Greeks pronounced their Greek. It is all theory, isn't it, assumptions from the Byzantine, probably quite wrong. . . ." He made a dismissive gesture.

To the boys it looked as if their teacher were about to contradict the Head. Surely he, if anyone, must know all there is to be known about the pronunciation of classical Greek, Franz thought, recalling the long-winded lectures in which the teacher had expounded on some types he called humanists. But Kandlbinder refrained from enlarging upon his knowledge in the presence of the Head. What a miserable coward! thought Franz. All Kandlbinder could manage to utter was a low, cautious: "But the double consonants—"

"—may possibly have been phonetically clarified," the Head completed the sentence. "I'll concede that." He paused briefly before sweeping this whole business of double consonants—long since dealt with by the class and much too easy for a star pupil—out of the way. "Besides, the class has gone far beyond the classification of sounds," he went on. "And it really would be deplorable if your students were still at the alphabet stage six weeks after Easter, wouldn't it, Dr. Kandlbinder? At alpha and omega!"

He gave a short, dry laugh that brought no change to his expression. "You have been doing pronunciation, syllables, and accents for some time now." Once again he laughed his expressionless laugh. "Proclitics and enclitics! Very good, very good! I see you have even started on syntax, Dr. Kandlbinder, with the infinitive. You have really advanced quite rapidly—my congratulations!"

Pretty embarrassing for that tedious fellow, thought

Franz, the way the Head has seen through him right away and told him to his face just where we stand in Greek. Although his words were those of praise, they sounded like the first far-off rumblings of an approaching thunderstorm. At least that was how they seemed to Franz. There could be no further doubt; the Head had taken over the lesson. From this moment on, Kandlbinder would be what he already was as he stood beside Schröter at the blackboard—no more than a marginal figure.

Schröter had turned away from the board to face the Head, politely and quietly awaiting the complex problems he would now presumably be set. Werner is tops, thought Franz; certainly no eager beaver, just someone who is simply able to do anything, and who can't help being that way. Franz Kien knew Werner Schröter better than most of the others did, he and Schröter being the only two boys in the class who were taking the violin lessons offered by the school as an elective. Two afternoons a week they and a few students from other classes met in the music room. They were now doing the third position. Werner produced a fuller tone than Franz; maybe he has a better violin than mine, thought Franz. But when he watched Werner tucking the instrument between his shoulder and chin, observed the concentration and intelligence in his expression, he realized that there was more to it than just the violin if some sequence of notes they were practicing sounded less scratchy as Werner played them.

Schröter wasn't tall, but he wasn't short either, and without being stocky he was sturdily built. There was a firmness even in his face. His smooth black hair swept over the upper part of his forehead in a semicircle; his eyebrows were black and thick. His nose, although broad-based, wasn't fleshy and was set in clean-cut lines below the dark-blue eyes, above the firm, straight mouth that he seldom used for talking. Although taciturn, he was always ready to help: if he noticed Franz having persistent trouble with his fingering, he would spontaneously walk over to him and, without saying a word or being in the least patronizing, place Franz's finger on the exact spot on the string that would cause the correct note to sound from the body of the violin. With his brown, firm hands he had also once moved the bridge on Franz's instrument by a fraction of a millimeter so that for a while the violin had sounded more beautiful than before.

Franz was disappointed in the music lessons; this practicing in the first position brought none of the pleasure he had hoped for. He hadn't imagined that a violin, without an accompanying instrument, would sound so dry, so inexpressive, really. If only I could have studied the piano, like Karl, he thought, but during the last two years—1927, 1928—his ailing father had no longer been able to afford a piano teacher. Karl had still benefited from the good times, Franz often thought enviously; in my case, there was only enough for these violin lessons—why do I say, "enough," they don't cost a thing, the school doesn't charge a cent for them, and the violin was a gift from the Poschenrieders, who happened to have one up in the attic. God, what a fuss they had made when they forked it over, acting as if the fiddle were a sacred object merely because their deceased son had played it.

The Head diverted him from reminiscences of his parents' friends, the Poschenrieders, who lived in a dark, elegant apartment on Sophien-Strasse and whom it was nesessary to visit some Sunday afternoons even when the weather was fine. Franz noted that the Head was paying no attention to Schröter. He totally ignored the student at the blackboard who was courteously but not obsequiously awaiting the wishes of His High and Mightiness. Instead he resumed his criticism of the pronunciation rules prevailing in these lessons, pretending to be talking to himself while still immersed in the grammar. "Musical accent!" he read out, while taking pains to suppress a scornful laugh. "The stressed syllable differs from the unstressed by a higher pitch."

Suddenly he turned toward the class. "Don't believe everything it says in here!" he exclaimed, pointing emphatically with his right index finger at the book he still held raised in his left hand. "At least not as gospel truth!" He paused, then continued: "Ah yes, if the Greeks had only known the phonograph. . . ."

Again he lapsed into contemplation, then remarked to Kandlbinder in a reverent tone: "A phonograph record with the voice of Socrates—that would be the greatest thing imaginable, don't you agree, Dr. Kandlbinder?"

No suitable reply occurred to the teacher, who merely nodded deferentially, as he did to all the Head's utterances. Probably he was just waiting for a chance to get on—finally—with the demonstration of Schröter's knowledge.

Was Franz mistaken, or did the Head genuinely have no interest in Schröter? Not only no interest but no real liking for him—it almost looks as if he doesn't much care for Schröter, thought Franz. Well, maybe I'm just imagining that—why should he have anything against him? But certainly he didn't turn even a little toward Schröter when Schröter turned toward him. Does he merely want to put an end to this stupid performance by the star pupil, or does he dislike Schröter? At least he could say something nice to him! But no friendly word issued from the Head's lips, and the dark-haired, sturdy, courteous boy promptly placed his piece of chalk on the shelf below the blackboard and returned to his seat when he heard the Head say, as he looked inquiringly around the room: "Now I would like to hear one of your other students, Dr. Kandlbinder!"

His tone was no longer affable. The father of the school taking an interest in one of his classes: that was definitely over. Now the man sitting up there behind the desk was a hunter stalking his prey in the classroom: one of those heavyset men who owned shooting rights and were first-class shots. The thirty Grade-8 boys sitting in pairs in three rows—the last rows of desks were empty—cowered. Not a chance that Kandlbinder will call on me, thought Franz, without wondering what made him so confident that his name wouldn't be mentioned during this period. Of course, Konrad, he thought with relief on turning around to see who the teacher was pointing at. He's calling on one model student after another—no danger of his picking me. When Kandlbinder said: "Come up to the front, will you?" Franz watched the boy who had been singled out jump to his feet from the last bench on the right. He wondered whether the Head had noticed that Kandlbinder avoided addressing this student by name.

The very manner in which the boy stood up—

quickly but not eagerly, lending the whole movement an air of absurdity by his exaggeratedly erect posture—gave the class reason to hope that some fun was in the offing. Nor did they have to wait more than a second or two: this loose-limbed youth, tall for his age, declared "With pleasure, Dr. Kandlbinder!" as he strolled with lackadaisical impudence between the rows of benches toward the blackboard, obviously out to enjoy himself.

To mimic the Head by addressing his teacher with the newly divulged title and by name—in fact, instead of obeying the order in silence, to answer it with that carefully planned and executed caricature of politeness, "With pleasure"—was yet another typical Konrad Greiff impertinence. The boys grinned.

One to nothing for Konrad, thought Franz; serves Kandlbinder right for calling on him merely because he's almost better in Greek than Werner Schröter. Kandlbinder is a dope; he must've imagined that Konrad would restrain himself while the Head was inspecting the class, but he's made a big mistake: the very fact that the Head is here is reason enough for him to show off again, like that time weeks ago when Kandlbinder called him for the first time. "Greiff," he had said, in all innocence, and Konrad had stood up—not as mockingly as today but arrogantly—and said to Kandlbinder in a voice of icy insolence: *"Von* Greiff, if you please!" Kandlbinder had been beside himself. His face had turned chalk-white; then he had shouted "This is outrageous!" and rushed out of the classroom, returning only after a longish interval. From then on he had rarely called upon Konrad, even though Konrad kept putting up his hand and in all his Greek assignments received an A or an A-minus. Never again did Kandlbinder address him by name.

Thus did Konrad completely unnerve the teacher. But why, after all, seeing that he doesn't insist on *our* addressing him as *von* Greiff? He knows we don't care two hoots about his *von*—we call him Greiff or Konrad, and he cheerfully puts up with it. It's really a dirty trick, taking this opportunity to show the Head what liberties he can take with their teacher! How could Kandlbinder not have foreseen this but instead actually have called upon him! This was the very time he should have stuck to his principle of never showing favoritism or any particular dislike, instead of which he calls first upon the star student and then on the only boy whom he certainly hates, though he never showed it again after Greiff had insisted he call him "von Greiff." I'd like to know what he did after rushing out of the classroom when that happened: Did he complain to the Head and ask him what to do about it, or did he run to the washroom to throw up? Konrad had still been standing there when he came back: all

Kandlbinder said to him was, "Sit down!" and from that moment on he never again addressed him by name. All the more idiotic to have called upon him now: the nitwit counted on Konrad's behaving decently toward him today. But Konrad has no such intention; he is obsessed with humiliating his teacher in front of the Head. But why? What a lousy aristocrat! His impudent "With pleasure, Dr. Kandlbinder!" was intended simply to make his teacher lose self-control, perhaps to be driven to a "Greiff, how dare you!" which would have finally given Konrad the desired opportunity—and in the presence of the Head—of getting in his *'von* Greiff, if you please!"

The entire class was already gleefully anticipating the verbal exchange that was about to follow. No doubt this too would end to the disadvantage of their teacher. Pitilessly the boys watched Kandlbinder submitting to this provocation as he stood, pale-faced and speechless, at the blackboard. But they had reckoned without the Head, who intervened at this point with a lightning speed Franz would never have expected from such a corpulent man.

"Ah!" he exclaimed, his blue-gold eyes coldly measuring Konrad, who had meanwhile reached the dais. "So here we have our young Baron Greiff! I have already heard a good deal about you, Greiff. You are said to be an excellent Greek scholar. But if you ever again find it necessary to express your willingness to obey an order, or if you ever again have the impertinence to address your teacher as 'Dr. Kandlbinder' instead of, as is fitting for you, 'Professor,' I shall punish you on the spot with an hour's detention. Is that clear, Greiff?"

So the Head knows Greiff, thought Franz. Then Kandlbinder, at the time of his confrontation with Konrad, must have rushed to him to complain about Konrad. Or does he know us all? He must really be on his toes if he knows every single one of us. By name and everything.

The way he dealt with Greiff! At that moment the entire class admired the Head. He had used the same method as with Kandlbinder. Just as he had produced the man's doctor title to create more respect for him, so he also first elevated Konrad Greiff's rank, making it clear to the class that in Konrad they had no mere common-or-garden *von* in their midst but something better, a baron after all. Yet while continuing to uphold their teacher's academic status—"Don't you agree, Dr. Kandlbinder?"—at least until now, and apart from pointing out to him, with a growling edge to his voice, that he shouldn't try to pull the wool over his eyes on the subject of teaching material—he had twice, right after addressing Konrad as "Baron," called him simply by his surname with no aristocratic handle.

Would Konrad dare to dress down the Head the way he had their teacher, six weeks earlier?

He seemed ready to take that risk. "Yet you yourself . . . ," he began, but the Head wouldn't let him finish.

"Very well then," he said calmly, without raising his voice. "One hour's detention. This afternoon, from three to four." He turned to Kandlbinder. "I'm sorry, Dr. Kandlbinder, to have to spoil your afternoon," he said, implying that the teacher would have to supervise the detention period. "But a gentleman of this type must not be allowed to get away with anything." He gave a sudden laugh. "A baron, indeed! See that he bones up on history this afternoon," he added. "He is not nearly as good in history as in Greek." He shook his head. "Strange, really, that someone so proud of his nobility should take so little interest in history."

He's completely informed about Konrad, thought Franz; he even knows how he's doing in other subjects. Franz observed the scene: the Head, who was obviously relishing the class's amazement that he was so thoroughly informed about Greiff; and Greiff, who had abandoned his nonchalant pose—his face was flushed—he hadn't reckoned with that hour's detention, thought Franz.

Once again the Head turned his attention to the boy

he was punishing. Patiently, but also with some viciousness, it seemed to Franz, the Head enlightened him. "What you were about to say, Greiff" again he used the name without prefix—"was that I myself addressed your homeroom teacher as 'Dr. Kandlbinder.' Perhaps I might have let you finish if, as would have been proper, you had said to me, 'Yet you yourself, Headmaster,' because for you I am not someone whom you address merely with 'you.' I am still your Headmaster, remember that. It is a shame that we are no longer permitted a conscript army in Germany. There you would learn that there is no such thing as 'yes' but only 'yessir!' Ah," he said, "they would certainly teach you the meaning of discipline there!"

How illogical, thought Franz. Even if we did have a proper army, not just this Reichswehr of a hundred thousand men the British and French allow us to keep, we would have already left school by the time we learned that you don't simply say "yes" to a lieutenant but "yessir!" We're only fourteen, after all. And although Franz also wished Germany had a proper army because his father had been an officer during the war, he didn't much like the idea of the kind of army life reflected in the Headmaster's tone. Had the Head also been at the front, he wondered, like my father, who was wounded three times? He couldn't imagine it; the Head didn't look like a front-line soldier, in fact not even like someone who had ever been wounded.

"I hope that one day each of you will have to serve in the armed forces," the Head continued, turning toward the whole class. "I hope the Reich will soon be strong enough again." But then almost without transition he moved from his military musings back to Konrad Greiff.

"But even had you addressed me correctly by my title," he said, "I would not have permitted you to address your teacher in the same manner as I do." Had all those subjunctives and conditionals exhausted him? In any case he sounded even a shade more casual than before when he added: "Your addressing the professor by name was particularly unseemly. 'Kandl-binder'!" he quoted. "Tsk, tsk, tsk! For that alone you would have deserved the hour's detention."

He had gone on a little too long and a little too pedantically about Konrad's breach of etiquette and seemed determined to overlook the condition into which he had driven the boy; even the back of Konrad's neck has turned crimson, thought Franz. Once again the tsk-tsk-tsk had sounded as if after that there was nothing more to be said: after that tongue-clicking, the Greiff case had been recognized and dismissed as hopeless. Really no need for him to keep on babbling, thought Franz. But the Head wasn't finished yet and couldn't refrain from adding: *"Quod licet Jovi, non licet bovi,* as you have no doubt learned in Latin!" He mouthed the maxim in a relaxed, almost leisurely tone, as if he had all the time in the world for homilies. Has he still not noticed, thought Franz, that he's provoking Konrad beyond endurance? They were all looking at their classmate, whose last vestiges of lofty scorn had by now been wiped out. There he stood, legs apart, and they could see his hands clenching tensely behind his back. Then it happened.

"I am not an ox!" he burst out. "And you are not Jupiter! Not for me! I am a Baron von Greiff, and as far as I am concerned you are nothing but a Mr. Himmler!"

That was more than the class had expected. In the wan light of the classroon now hung the pale shrouds of immobility and deathly silence; even the rays of early-summer light from the chestnut tree outside in the school playground suddenly refracted on the windowpanes and no longer entered the room. Only the Head's imminent outburst would release the boys from the tension in which they were locked; they waited breathlessly to see what form his loss of self-control would take.

They were disappointed. The Head maintained his composure, did not blaze up in a rage—what fantastic self-control, thought Franz. With inimitable calm he shook his massive head with its cap of thin white hair; his face, still smooth in spite of his age, did not even change color. Only the way he finally put down the Greek grammar—soundlessly, warily, decisively— told them he was not going to let Konrad Greiff get away with that personal insult, that outrageous impudence: in the entire history of the *Gymnasium*, which bore the name of the Bavarian royal house, nothing like this had ever happened before.

However, at first he merely displayed his expertise, that of the scholar who chose as a hobby to teach history to the graduating class, although as Headmaster he was under no obligation to teach at all.

"As for your nobility," he began, "it is not worth as much as you may think, Greiff. Greiff," he repeated, actually managing to assume a tone of superior objectivity, "is in fact simply a surname that many knights chose to assume. Greif, Grif, Grip—that's how those fellows called themselves, after the legendary bird of prey, the griffin. Most of them had originally been mere nameless exploiters of peasants appointed by a feudal lord as overseers of some of his villages. Their descendants became robber barons, those Greiffs, adding some regional name: Greiff von such-and-such. In the case of your family, the Greiffs from Lower Franconia, they didn't even manage that much."

Only when he spoke of "those fellows" had his

voice momentarily lost its objectivity, turned vicious.
But not until he had claimed that Konrad's ancestors
had in fact been nameless did he cease his loathsome
homilies and begin to take revenge on Greiff for telling him he was, as far as Konrad was concerned,
"nothing but a Mr. Himmler." And even then the
Head tried to appear relaxed—what an actor! thought
Franz, suddenly filled with hatred as he heard the
Head asking: "Do you know who once explained all
this very clearly to me, Greiff? Your father! I have
occasionally had the pleasure of a conversation with
him. He is a man of very sound opinions, not in the
least vain of his aristocratic title."

With revolting affability he's given Konrad a slap in
the face, thought Franz. So it can really happen, that
one person can slap the face of another person with
such revolting affability. He shot a glance at Hugo
Aletter to see whether Hugo felt as outraged as he did,
but Hugo's pale face betrayed nothing: he was merely
gazing spellbound at the scene unfolding by the
teacher's desk, and even Konrad didn't seem aware of
any slap or, if he was, he brusquely shook it off. His
rage seemed to be already spent; the hands clenched
behind his back unclasped. He found his voice again.

"My father always likes to appear modest," he proceeded to inform the Head with icy scorn. "He's a real
expert at that. But in reality. . . ." He left the sen-

tence dangling, merely shrugging as he continued: "We have two castles, three hundred hectares of fields under cultivation, and three hundred hectares of forest."

"I know some of your father's peers who own three thousand hectares of property," countered the Head, anxious not to be outdone; but it didn't come off, he could no longer hide his anger. He's angry not at what Konrad said but that Konrad said anything at all, thought Franz. Because in school it is simply unheard of for a student to contradict his teacher—and the Head, of all people!—and not only contradict him but behave as if he could talk to his teacher just as he would to anybody else. Terrific, the way Konrad brought that off! The Head should have brushed aside that insolent boasting about castles and fields and forests with a wave of his hand. Instead he had allowed himself to get embroiled in a verbal tussle with Konrad and even now was still unable to extricate himself.

"Your castles are not so old," argued the Head, who may already have known that he had lost the game. "Sixteenth century!" he said, his tone implying that that was nothing. And he even yielded to the temptation to go one better. "We Himmlers are much older." He raised his right index finger. "Documentary proof of an ancient city-patriciate from the Upper Rhine. A

Himmler House in Basel and one in Mainz! The one
in Basel bears the date 1297!"

"Congratulations!" said Konrad.

Probably he knew no more than all the others what
that was: "city-patriciate." In the history lessons they
had had so far, from Grades 6 to 8, that expression had
never come up. Franz was bored by history lessons.
He had no desire to learn by heart the dates of battles
in which, so they were taught, the fate of nations or
great men was decided. "City-patriciate," the way the
Head said it, must be something important, something like "aristocracy," which of course Konrad von
Greiff could not accept. For him there was nothing fit
even to hold a candle to the aristocracy. But he was in
no position to argue with the Head about an unfamiliar
expression, thought Franz, and by this time he simply
no longer cares since he knows for sure that he can
never atone for his insult of addressing the Head by
name. He has ignored the most basic of all school
rules: Teachers don't have names, they have titles,
and between teacher and student there is no such
thing as "Mr. Kandlbinder," only "Professor." Besides, not satisfied with merely addressing the Head
by name, Konrad had expressly stated that, as far as he
was concerned, the Head was *nothing but* that name,
Himmler, an insult too grave ever to be wiped out.

Konrad has ceased to care about anything, even the consequences; his only desire now is to see how far he can go. Kandlbinder's through with him anyway, and now the Head is too, irrevocably. In fact Konrad is no longer risking anything by insolently congratulating the Head on his "city-patriciate."

"Congratulations!" That really was the limit! That was the last straw.

Their teacher, a mere shadow by the blackboard during the entire scene, now finally made a move as if wanting to intervene, to come to the aid of his superior, perhaps to cry out something like: "That's outrageous!" But this time, too, he was forestalled by the Head, who was now left with only one recourse: to exact retribution. He can't possibly let that "Congratulations!" go unchallenged, thought Franz, and once again he admired the Head for not exploding but remaining calm, displaying no emotion.

"Well," he said, adopting an indifferent, almost weary tone, "this boy seems to be beyond redemption." And then he pronounced the verdict, one that must surely have been decided upon the moment Konrad Greiff had described him as "nothing but a Mr. Himmler."

"I shall write a letter to your father and ask him to remove you from the school," he said. "From what I know of him, he will not rejoice at that. But he will realize that in my school there is no room for a lout such as you."

His school, thought Franz. As if he owned it! It's just a school like any other. Yet he talks about *his* school, about *my* Grade 8-B that he can do whatever he likes with.

So Konrad was being expelled, although he was an "excellent Greek scholar" but also such an insolent bastard that the Head couldn't cope with him. It was the first time they had ever been present at the expulsion of a student. For them, the word "expulsion" was merely the dark threat of a punishment so severe that it was never carried out.

Since Konrad was still standing with his back to the class, Franz couldn't make out how his expulsion was affecting him. Apparently not at all, for his speech didn't desert him even for a moment. On the contrary, they heard him ask, promptly and almost cheerfully: "In that case, then, I won't have to serve an hour's detention this afternoon, will I, Headmaster?"

With this he finally succeeded in exhausting the Headmaster's patience—the genuine or the assumed, went through Franz's mind. The Headmaster rose to his feet behind the desk and barked at the boy. "Sit down, Greiff! You will wait for any other information the school may have to give you. Until then you will follow its rules."

They saw Konrad hesitate a moment, then, with a shrug, obey the order. His look seemed to imply: "The wiser head gives in." But he really no longer needs to give in, thought Franz. He's been kicked out, he could pick up his books and leave. But Konrad merely turned and went back to his seat, only the twisted smile on his face betraying that he didn't feel entirely victorious, although actually he had emerged from this duel as the winner.

The Head did not resume his seat. Stepping down from behind the desk, he stood for a while with their teacher while the two men whispered together. They must be talking about Konrad, thought Franz. The Head is instructing Kandlbinder how to deal with Konrad for as long as he stays in school. The tension now being over, the class was becoming restless, and the Head let it pass, but silence fell again as soon as he began to walk up and down between the rows of desks, a corpulent man in a light-weight, pale-gray suit, jacket unbuttoned. The white shirt bulged over his paunch, the blue tie, immaculately knotted and in place, was still shiny, and behind the spectacles with their thin gold rims the blue eyes looked out affably, even benevolently. The chestnut tree in the playground filtered the light of a fine May day through the closed windowpanes of the classroom. Munich shone, the Head shone, yet the whole class thought what

Franz was thinking: Now he's looking for a new victim. He no longer leaves it to Kandlbinder to call upon the students. Holy smoke, thought Franz with a jolt, it might even be his own turn. It was a shock to realize that old Himmler might summon *him* to the blackboard to test him in Greek.

For quite a while he had already been thinking "old Himmler" instead of "the Head," because the moment Konrad Greiff had given the great man a name—just as you don't call a dog "Dog" but "Hector" or "Fido"—he had remembered how, the day he had entered the *Gymnasium*, he had been warned by his father about the head of the school.

"The headmaster of the Wittelsbach *Gymnasium* is old Himmler," he had said. "Watch out for him! Not that you'll have much contact with him, especially in the lower grades, but, if you should, be sure you don't get on the wrong side of him! The man is dangerous!"

That had been three years ago, and meanwhile the title had pushed itself in front of the name. For the whole school the Head was the Head, and nothing more: it seemed that only for Konrad Greiff was he nothing but a Mr. Himmler. Incidentally, his father had never explained why he considered the "man" to be dangerous. Franz had wondered why he had called him "old Himmler"; after all, the Head was at most only a few years older than Father! But before he could ask him about this an answer came in the form of a comparison, for his father mentioned a "young Himmler" who was the Headmaster's son.

"There's nothing wrong with young Himmler," his father had told him. "A splendid young man, a follower of Hitler, but not hidebound—he always comes to our Ludendorff rallies as well, and to 'Reich Banner' meetings, too. Among the young fellows who come to our meetings he's the smartest and most reliable—cool-headed, but with an iron will. Since he was born in 1900 he was too young to fight in the war, but I am sure that in the trenches he would have proved his mettle; I would have been happy to have anyone like him in my company. He and his father have become mortal enemies—his father's a member of the Bavarian People's Party, Catholic to the core, though he considers himself a nationalist. But in the war he was never anywhere near the front lines, and he's not even anti-Semitic, thinks nothing of associating with Jews—just imagine, with Jews! That's why his son broke off all relations with him—young Himmler would never sit at the same table with Jews, Jesuits, or Freemasons.

"Old Himmler is a careerist," he added. "Beware of careerists in your life, my son!" he said solemnly. "Every Sunday he goes to High Mass at St. Michael's on Kaufinger-Strasse, where you can see them all together, those people who aspire to belonging to the cream of Munich society."

How does he know that? Franz had wondered while listening to this explanation. Father's a Protestant; as far as I know he's never attended a Catholic mass. The Kiens were a Protestant family; his mother had been expelled from the Catholic Church for marrying a Protestant and allowing her children to be baptized as Protestants, which Father had insisted upon. Franz Kien senior—Franz had been baptized with his father's given name—was not only a Ludendorff follower and an anti-Semite but also a devout Lutheran. Until Franz was confirmed, he recalled, he was sent every Sunday to the children's service at Christ Church.

At that time, three years ago, his father had still talked to his son with animation and passion about the doctrines of his idol General Ludendorff, in a metallic voice that brooked no contradictions and matched his fiery-red face under the black hair. Franz was invariably impressed as he listened to that voice—only later did doubts, objections, arise in him. Now, three years later, that voice had lost its vibrancy. To Franz, his father now seemed a broken man: his disease had changed him. He spent a lot of time lying down, his business affairs were going badly, and he no longer wore his captain's uniform when, still erect but in mufti, he attended one of those nationalistic military ceremonies that took place in Munich on every conceivable occasion. Only the tiny rosette in the buttonhole of his civilian suit testified to his having been seriously wounded in the war and awarded the Iron Cross First Class.

Walking up and down between the rows of desks, the Head didn't look like someone who had ever been awarded a ribbon for a war wound. He looks healthy, thought Franz, fat and healthy, even though he's not one of those jolly fat people. He doesn't look ill like Father, yet he must be at least ten years older than Father, not just a few years as I had imagined—he's probably sixty if he has a son who is twice as old as I am and already active in politics. In any case, old Himmler looks well preserved; only from close up can you see that his face isn't unlined but a mass of tiny wrinkles. Still, his skin appears smooth, lightly flushed as it is, a pale flesh-pink below the smooth white hair. Everything about him is pale, smooth, unctuous, as immaculate as his white shirt, but I don't like him. My sick father, who no longer looks as proud as he used to, is more to my liking, even when he flies into one of his rages and yells at me for getting another F on a math test, though I can't help being no good at math. And I still prefer that pale-faced, boring Kandlbinder to this repulsive Mr. Bigshot. Not for anything would I want

to be his son, I can understand his son having a row
with him and leaving home if he always had to listen to
all that stuff about Socrates—that a phonograph record
with the voice of Socrates would be the greatest thing
imaginable. And how about Socrates gurgling down
that hemlock juice—would old Himmler want to listen
to that too? Franz wouldn't put it past him. Or Christ
on the Cross, the Last Words—Franz's imagination
grew more and more extravagant—wouldn't that be
what the Headmaster, Catholic to the core as his father claimed, would listen to over and over again—
assuming that in those days they could have recorded
that "Father, Father, why hast Thou forsaken me?"

On the other hand, the Head was a man who could
point emphatically at the Greek grammar and declare:
"Don't believe everything it says in here!" Venerate
Socrates and dispute the grammar—how could he find
room for both in his head? Either he had a larger skull
than the other teachers—Kandlbinder, for example—
or he was simply a bit gaga.

Now he was coming along the aisle where Franz
Kien was sitting; he halted beside him. Franz didn't
look up. Keeping his head down, he was aware only of
the taut white shirt over the paunch at his side, and of
a hand on which tiny white—or were they blond?—
hairs shimmered over a few brown liver spots. The
Head wore a wide gold wedding band on the ring

finger of his right hand. Franz noted all these things in
the desperate hope that the Head might not be sin-
gling him out, although he had stopped beside Franz
on his prowl—a hunter who has heard a twig cracking
in the undergrowth.

And indeed the fervent prayer expressed in Franz's
fixed gaze away from the Head's face did seem to have
helped somewhat, for the Head turned not to Franz
but to Hugo Aletter sitting beside Franz—not to test
him but merely to point his hand with its gleaming
gold ring, past Franz's face, at Hugo.

"Remove that badge from your jacket this instant!"
he said sharply.

A few weeks earlier, Hugo had cut out a swastika
from a thin sheet of gilt metal. It had turned out quite
well, and he wore it proudly on the lapel of his jacket.
Not that it had much significance, as Franz was aware;
Hugo wore it only because he liked the symbol, and
because his parents who, like almost all the *Gymnasium*
boys' parents, supported the German National Party,
saw nothing wrong with it. Of course, if he had managed to get hold of a real Hitler party badge, a round
enamelled thing, they would have taken it away from
him. They would have seen that as going too far and
not appropriate to his age, but that little homemade
object they let him keep—it was only a symbol, a
youngster's whim.

Franz, relieved that the Head's attention was not directed at him after all, glanced at Hugo. He noticed Hugo's pale, spotty face change color and saw him hastily obey by unfastening the swastika from his lapel and putting it in his jacket pocket.

The Head lowered his arm and turned toward the homeroom teacher, who seemed unable to tear himself away from his place at the blackboard. He stands there as if glued to the spot, thought Franz.

"No doubt you are aware, Mr. Kandlbinder," he said, "that I do not wish to see any political badges in my school."

He had dropped all pretense at courtesy and no longer addressed the teacher as "Doctor."

"I have constantly reminded the students of that," Kandlbinder replied.

"Tsk, tsk, tsk!" At last the Head had found another opportunity to produce his famous tongue-clicking that precluded all further discussion and always sounded like the cracking of a whip. "So I will put another notice on the bulletin board. Why must one always repeat everything! No political badges!" he proclaimed over the heads of the students. "Preferably no badges at all! Let that be a warning!"

It sounded convincing. So in prohibiting political badges he meant not only Hugo's swastika but badges of any kind. Although the swastika must be partic-

ularly galling to him, thought Franz, because he
blames it for the rift with his son, for their being in fact
mortal enemies, as Father had put it. They no longer
had anything to do with each other, old Himmler and
his son. Still, Franz doubted whether the Head's son
had broken with his father merely because he had
joined the swastika crowd. It might have been because
the old man was such a pain in the ass that he couldn't
stand being around him any more.

But then the Head supplied an explanation for his
outlawing of badges that was simply unanswerable.

"If I permit that thing," he said, pointing once
again at the now empty lapel of Hugo's jacket, "I can
do nothing about someone who turns up at school one
day wearing the Soviet star. But then of course," he
added, "such a person would be out on his ear in no
time."

Sure, thought Franz. Confronted by a Soviet star,
the Head couldn't be content with saying: "Take it
off!" In that case he would have to change his tune,
although Franz knew nobody in the class, in fact not a
single student or teacher in the entire school, who
could ever be suspected of being a Bolshie. That was
unthinkable. How could the Head even imagine such
a thing! But then of course he does think of everything.

There were quite a few swastika followers among

the students, but there were also a few Jews. In Grade
8-B there was Georg Bernstein, Georg was a great guy.
In winter he would go skiing with them, and he'd
taught them a terrific technique of attaching the skins
to the skis that made going uphill easier. And the way
he managed the Brauneck run, which was so steep and
narrow—like a champ—you just didn't notice that
Georg Bernstein was a Jew, and anyway his parents
were just as loyal German Nationalists as almost all the
other parents. Franz had once mentioned this to his
father, whose response had been: "Yes, I know, there
are a few decent Jews, but be on your guard there,
too!"

In that respect Franz couldn't agree with his
father—it was obviously nonsense—Mr. Bernstein
had fought at the front during the war, just like his
own father, and he also had the Iron Cross First Class.
Franz saw no reason to be on his guard when Georg
explained the advantages of his old-fashioned Bilgeri
binding as they walked, drenched with sweat from the
downhill run, through the streets of Lenggries. Would
the younger Himmler maybe change his attitude toward the Jews if he came in contact with more Jews
like Georg Bernstein? Franz thought he might, wished
he would, because he felt he liked the younger
Himmler although he had never met him. A son who
had turned his back on that father, on that ancient,

worn-out, scratchy Socrates-record, must have something going for him. The only thing Franz didn't ap-
prove of was his taking up with that anti-Semitic Mr.
Hitler, as if Hitler could be a new father to him. Franz
had seen pictures of Hitler—Hitler had a face that
didn't interest him. He looked stupid and mediocre.
Here Franz had to side with old Himmler, who
wouldn't tolerate the swastika at the Wittelsbach
Gymnasium—he obviously had to prevent Hugo Aletter and Georg Bernstein, say, beating each other up—
and without for an instant admitting that this was his
reason for coming down so hard on Hugo. There were
already too many swastika devotees in the school the
Head would rather not tangle with, so he preferred to
use the Soviet star argument where nobody could contradict him and he could still hide the fact that he had
a special account to settle with the swastika.

But at that moment Franz Kien's thoughts suddenly
come to a standstill: the Head dropped the hand that
had just been directed at Hugo Aletter onto Franz's
shoulder as he asked: "Well, Kien, what can you
tell us about your Greek?" He stressed the word
"your."

Impossible, thought Franz. This couldn't happen.
But the next moment: It has happened. It's happen-
ing. The Head's going to test me in Greek. Oh God
Almighty. Lord God Almighty. A disaster. A real

disaster. This must be what it's like to be run over by a car. Out of the blue you're hit by a heavy metal object and flung onto the street. Sit down again, I'd rather ask someone else—those words would not be uttered; they were no more than a wild, flickering hope, quickly extinguished after Franz had risen, for whenever a student was addressed by a teacher he had to stand up. So Franz was standing beside the bench, being so tall for his age that there wasn't room for him to stand between bench and desk. He knew he needn't answer the question about his Greek, in fact wasn't even allowed to answer. Besides, he couldn't possibly have answered it, so dazed was he at that moment by the enormity that was descending on him like a veil. His eyes actually felt dim, his vision narrowed, and he was scarcely aware of the gleeful expressions of the other boys turning toward him.

The question about his Greek had been put quite amiably, as if the Head were only mildly interested in hearing how Franz was coping with classical Greek. But then his voice assumed a sharper edge as he added: "I hope you've worked a little harder at Greek than at Latin, in which you have not exactly covered yourself with glory."

Thus he demonstrated to the whole class that he was as fully informed on Franz Kien's performance as on Konrad Greiff's. He must be checking the reports of each student before inspecting a class and selecting in advance the ones he's going to single out. He didn't mind the class knowing that he left nothing to chance, that he had carefully prepared himself for the encounter—in fact he intended them to realize this.

Franz remained standing. There was a chance, after all, that the Head would not summon him to the blackboard but be satisfied with a few oral answers. And for a brief instant he hoped that by some miracle he might escape the whole ordeal when the Head said, although with a mean little smile: "It is meritorious to extol Franz Kien."

Franz, gaping in astonishment, stared at him as if at an apparition. What's he getting at? he thought. We haven't had any sentence with my name in it! He's pulling my leg, he wants to play me for a sucker.

"You seem surprised," the Head continued. "Be good enough to write that sentence on the blackboard! In Greek, of course. It has come up in the last or last-but-one lesson"—he half turned toward Kandlbinder, who called out: "Last Tuesday!"—"as one of the simplest examples of the use of the infinitive," the Head went on. "The infinitive as a verbal noun of purpose. Do you know what a verbal noun is?"

Franz remained silent. Better to say nothing than the wrong thing, he thought, and the Head seemed of the same opinion. "Actually, there is no need for you to know," he said, then added: "But you must be able to do the sentence because it was one of your assignments for today."

And with upturned palm, a gesture that implied a courteous invitation but was in reality vicious and inexorable, he directed Franz to the blackboard. Mr. Kandlbinder stepped aside, exposing the dark, threatening surface, blank but for the symbols of the three double consonants that Werner Schröter had written in the upper left corner. The Head having little interest in star pupils, Werner had hurried back to his seat without wiping them off.

The Head followed Franz to the front—sneaking up behind me! thought Franz—but did not resume his seat at the desk. Instead he merely picked up the grammar, looked at the open page, and quoted from it, speaking in Kandlbinder's direction: "Adverbial of purpose with adjectives! Tsk, tsk, tsk—and fourteen-year-olds are supposed to make heads or tails of this! And then it also says: Supine II, or dative of purpose, or relative clause of result. It's enough to drive you up the wall!" His voice was now dripping with undisguised scorn. Appealing to the class, he called out: "Does anyone know what a relative clause of result is?" And when no hand went up he said, again to Kandlbinder: "You see? I don't even know it myself, at least I would have to think very hard about the possible meaning of a relative clause of result." He brought his hand down heavily on the book. "These authors of grammars!" he said angrily. "Because they write for use in humanist schools, they think they have to find a term to classify each and every thing!" He paused and shook his head. "It's high time," he went on, "for me to investigate whether there isn't a grammar that makes sense to eighth graders. A grammar that is clear and graphic. Teaching material must be clear and graphic—otherwise it's just so much dead weight."

Franz wasn't listening. He was absorbing just enough to be able to tell himself that for once he could completely agree with the Head. But he wasn't concentrating on the Head's rhetoric: he was merely glad the Head would ignore him as long as he was holding forth with his loud, carping monologue about the grammar.

It ended abruptly. The sharp blue eyes, framed in thin gold, were aimed at Franz, whose inspiration meanwhile had not gone beyond picking up a piece of chalk. Then the Head looked at the blackboard and asked in sanctimonious surprise: "What—no sentence yet? I thought you had written it long ago!"

Franz stood helplessly at the blackboard, half turned toward the Headmaster but looking at the floor. With an effort he called the sentence to mind but without any idea of what it looked like translated into Greek letters. Yes, we did have a sentence something like that on Tuesday, he remembered, but since then I've never looked at the grammar. With all that fine weather I spent every afternoon outside, and in the evenings I read Karl May—*Through Wildest Kurdistan.*

"It is meritorious to extol Franz Kien because he is a gifted and hard-working student," said the Head with visible relish. "Starting with the word 'because,' we have a relative clause of result, have we not, Dr. Kandlbinder?"

Franz couldn't see that the teacher, who was now standing by the classroom door, was wearing a sour-sweet smile. It was only from the Head's triumphant "You see? It's that simple!" that Franz could assume that Kandlbinder had agreed with his superior.

"Well then, get on with it!" the Head told Franz. "Don't hold up the works! You may dispense with 'Franz Kien,' of course. Simply write what is in the grammar: 'It is meritorious to extol the country!'"

Noticing that Franz had no idea where to start, he relented sufficiently to offer some help.

"Estin," he said.

"Of course," Franz muttered, in a vain attempt to

fool the Head into believing that what he had learned
had momentarily slipped his mind. Out it came, part
embarrassed, part deceitful: "Of course!"

He managed to write the word on the blackboard,
εστιν. Not a difficult word.

He lowered the hand that was holding the chalk and
stared earnestly at the blackboard, with the pretense
of thinking hard, concentrating, but he wasn't concentrating at all, and he knew there was no point in concentrating: he would never remember how the sentence went on. Never. Never ever.

"Try to speak the sentence if you don't know how
to write it!" the Head prompted him.

The only response was agonized silence. The Head
lost patience. "You were obviously asleep last Tuesday!" he said. Like hammer blows he pounded the
words of the sentence into Franz's ears and those of
the class.

*"Estin . . . axia . . . hēde . . . hē . . . khora . . .
epaineisthai."*

What with his utter confusion, with his continuing
shock at having been summoned for this Greek test,
had Franz even been listening? At least he had noted
that the word *estin* was followed by *axia*, and he managed to write it correctly by copying the double consonant left by Werner Schröter on the board. It re-

minded him just in time of the Greek way of writing X and prevented him from using the Latin form.

At the two words that had sounded like the bleating of a goat, "hei . . . hei," he hesitated. He took too long to remember that there was no H in Greek, and just as it came to him the Head chided: "In Greek there is no aspirate—you do know that, I hope!" Franz nodded. "Aha," said the Head, "so you don't know how to write *eta*." He stepped to the blackboard, picked up a piece of chalk, and wrote the two words ηδε and η. There they stood, firmly and confidently outlined, beside Franz's clumsily scrawled αξια.

How mean, thought Franz, two more seconds was all he needed to give me, and I'd have remembered the *eta*. I know the Greek alphabet pretty well, otherwise I couldn't more or less manage to write a sentence on the board that I've never bothered to learn. When we began Greek at Easter, I enjoyed learning the alphabet, the letters are beautiful, but then when we started sweating over grammar I suddenly lost all interest.

"I ought to send you back to your seat," said the Head. "It is already quite clear that you have learned nothing and know nothing. But we will go on a little, Kien—I am interested in ascertaining the extent of your laziness and ignorance."

So he doesn't even give me credit for writing—so far at least—the words correctly. Even *hēde* and *hē* I would have got right too, but when it came to the goat-bleatings, he was just too quick for me. He's determined to clobber me. He's like the Assistant Head Endres.

Assistant Head Endres taught math in Grade 8-B. He was a short, thick-set man with incredibly broad shoulders and a complexion that looked like tanned yellow leather. Once, when he was handing back a bunch of corrected assignments and Franz was expecting the inevitable F he got in math, he announced so that the whole class could hear him: "This time, by hook or by crook, Kien has actually managed to pull off a C!"

"Let us put a swift end to the tragedy!" said the Head. *"Khora . . . khora . . . khora,"* he dinned into Franz's ears, pronouncing the initial KH with a gutteral sound.

This time, too, Franz succeeded in finding the required symbol for KH.

χωρα, he wrote.

"Well, I never!" the Head scoffed. "What an achievement!" His tribute made it sound as if Franz had just learned how to add two and two. "Now all that's lacking is the *epainesthai*," he went on. "You'll have no trouble with that."

Hesitantly Franz set to work on the long word. He found it distracting for the Head to be speaking to the class while he was slowly writing letter after letter on the board.

"Epaineisthai," the Head held forth. That is actually the infinitive mentioned in the grammar. 'It is commendable to compliment the country,'" he translated, deftly making use of the alliteration that had just occurred to him. "But it is exactly the same in German. I cannot understand why your textbook implies that the Greeks had come up with some grammatical specialty here."

"But Headmaster!" Suddenly Kandlbinder spoke up with an indignant voice. Until this moment the entire class, mildly interested and mildly contemptuous, had observed their teacher being obliged to swallow in silence the fact that the Head, now no longer a mere observer, had taken over the instruction himself, thus depriving Kandlbinder of a chance to shine as a teacher. He had endured that slight without demur. But the Head's biased (so it seemed to Kandlbinder) fault-finding of the grammar was the last straw; it could not, must not, be allowed to pass. What do you know, thought Franz, Kandlbinder's getting on his hind legs! All ears, he listened to the expert in the teacher contriving to do what the man was by nature incapable of doing: contradicting a superior.

"But Headmaster!" said Kandlbinder, sounding not only indignant but downright offended. "In this case the text merely presupposes that the German adverbial form 'meritorious' is to be translated into Greek. And it points out that an adjective used as an adverbial to express purpose must be followed in Greek by the infinitive, whereas in German we could choose a variety of other possibilities."

Triumphantly he emphasized the "could," which in his opinion represented the final and most compelling element of the argument.

"Really—you think so?" replied the Head. He spoke meekly, in a tone of cautious doubt. He broke off, then in an unctuous voice resumed: "I am afraid, my dear colleague, that this is not the place to argue about the differences between adverb and adverbial, for that is what our conversation would amount to, would it not, Dr. Kandlbinder?"

Franz, having finished writing the infinitive under discussion, had turned around. He looked from the Head to his teacher—the Head considered himself victorious, whereas Kandlbinder was obviously wrestling with himself as to whether to continue the argument or, perhaps more wisely, keep his mouth shut. In the sentence that Franz had so laboriously but more or less correctly (though with prompting) scrawled on the blackboard, did *axia* represent an adverb or an

adverbial? He—Franz Kien—didn't give a damn. All
he wanted was for the argument between the two
teachers to be prolonged, preferably till the end of the
lesson, when the shrill sound of the bell in the corri-
dors would, as with one magic stroke, wipe out the
entire nightmare of this period.

However, the Head ended the confrontation by de-
claring: "Let's leave it at that. The subject will not
come up anyway until Grade 9."

He turned back toward Franz, shook his head as he
looked at the εηειvεισθει that Franz had written,
walked to the blackboard, picked up the cloth lying on
the shelf—still damp from Werner Schröter's use of
it—erased the "e's" after the "pi" and the "theta,"
and replaced them with "a's," so that finally, in a
mixture of such differing handwritings as Franz Kien's
and the Headmaster's—one inconsistent and sloppy
and one vigorous and betraying not a shred of self-
doubt—the word appeared correctly on the blackboard: εηαινεισθχι.

"I clearly enunciated the alternation of 'ai' and 'ei'
in the syllables," said the Head, "but you seem to be
incapable of even listening."

"You," he continued, and the way he stressed that
"you" left no doubt of his intention to exclude Franz
then and there from the class, from the fellowship of
his classmates. "You will not make it to Grade 9."

Franz gave a barely perceptible shrug. For the last few minutes he had no longer been sweating; in fact he felt cold. So the Head had given up on him. Not expelled, like Greiff, I've given him no cause for that, thought Franz. I'm not pig-headed like Greiff, but he's given up on me. The good thing is, he'll stop this testing and call someone else to the blackboard. If I'm going to repeat the year anyway, he needn't go on examining me.

Cheap shot, thought Franz. It was bound to come. The only reason for his picking that sentence is so he can turn it around and slap me down with it.

Once again the Head looked at the blackboard. "And yet you could if you wanted to," he said. "You just don't want to."

This comment was not new to Franz. He got to hear it at regular intervals from his father and from all his teachers. He was sick and tired of it. Hell, he thought, hell, hell, hell. Even supposing they're right, why doesn't anyone ask me *why* I don't want to?

I don't know myself, he thought.

The trouble was that the Head still wouldn't let go. Instead of finally waving him back to his seat, he asked: "Tell me—have you ever considered what you want to be?"

"A writer," replied Franz.

The Head pushed himself back from the desk he

had been leaning against, straightened up, and stared at Franz.

That's thrown him for a loop, thought Franz. He wasn't prepared for that. He believed that once again I would say nothing, just gape at him without a word. But I told him I want to be a writer because it's true. That's all I want to be: a writer.

"Huh?" the Head asked. This common, almost vulgar "huh" was the first sound he had uttered since Franz's declaration and sounded almost like the giggling from some of the benches. Then he regained control of himself and decided to be understanding, show kindness.

"So what do you imagine a writer to be?" he asked.

Franz raised his shoulders and dropped them again. "A person who writes books," he replied. Stupid question: he thinks that because I'm only fourteen I wouldn't know what a writer is.

"And what kind of books would you like to write?" the Head asked, in a tone that baffled Franz. Was he just dealing with a teenage boy who's slightly nuts, or could he be genuinely eager to know what I'm going to answer—in other words, take me seriously? That'd really be something, for the Head to take me seriously!

"I don't know yet," he answered.

When I'm older, I'll know, he thought. At eighteen

or twenty. He considered whether to tell the Head
that even as a little boy he had been writing, but of
course that was out of the question, here in front of the
class. The class would hoot with laughter. In his father's bookcase he had found an edition of Shakespeare and pored over it. King Henry IV. King Rich-
ard III. His father had a supply of yellow ruled
foolscap, and Franz had used these sheets to write
plays in the style of Shakespeare. Had he been eight
or nine or ten at the time? Still in elementary school or
already at the *Gymnasium?* But he managed to think of
himself as a little boy when he remembered such pas-
times, which he had kept secret from his parents and
brothers. Meanwhile he had come to the conviction
that he must wait to become a writer—to write now
would be childish.

"I see, you don't know yet," the Head said approv-
ingly. "Quite an intelligent answer—I would never
have expected it of you. I hope you are reading good
books. Have you any favorites?"

"Karl May," said Franz.

The Head recoiled in disgust. "That is enough to
ruin your imagination!" he cried. "Karl May is poison!"

This was exactly what Franz's father had said when
he caught him reading a book by Karl May. He had
taken the book away, just at the most thrilling point,

Winnetou's death, and it was two weeks before Franz was able to borrow a copy from a classmate and finish it. He had hated his father. "Karl May is poison"—they didn't know what they were talking about! He wouldn't stop reading Karl May. Maybe later. But not now.

The Head was so disappointed by the information he had received—what had he imagined? thought Franz, am I supposed to read Goethe or Schiller?—that he reverted, coldly and dispassionately, to the subject of Franz's failure in school.

"If you do indeed want to become a writer," he said, and this time, no longer bothering to restrain himself, he invested the word for Franz's intended profession with a maximum of scorn, "I fail to understand why you make no effort in languages. Latin! Greek! Surely you should be going at them heart and soul. Grammar! How can someone become a writer if he is not interested in grammar?" Involuntarily he had worked himself up from contempt to wrathful indignation.

Suddenly he's singing the praises of grammar, thought Franz, and earlier he was saying we shouldn't believe everything we see in the grammar. But then that's simply not the point: the point is that it's not only Latin and Greek I don't want to learn—I'm just not interested in learning anything. I'm no good at math, OK, I can't do anything about that, but in German and history and geography I could easily wangle better marks than those eternal C's I never get beyond. Even in biology I just sit there daydreaming, although I like old Professor Burckhardt, and he seems to like me too. Not even playing the violin can give me a kick—I'm bored to death by that scratching away in the lower positions, yet I'd been so much looking forward to it. Heart and soul? Not me. Not in school.

But why, why, why? Most of the others just learn their stuff and knock off their assignments, there are even a few who are just plain dumb—no matter how hard they try they can't make it, while Werner Schröter doesn't have to study anything, he knows it all anyway, it all comes easily to him. But I could if I wanted to. If they all say so, it must be true. But I don't want to. They all go on about "wanting." One just has to *want* to do something, and things will take care of themselves. If someone doesn't want to, he's lazy, and they're right, I am lazy. I sit half paralyzed over my homework and scribble something off the top of my head, or I put it off till the evening and go outside to play. I find school dreary, dreary, dreary! Burckhardt is the only one who sometimes says to me: "Kien, your thoughts are flying out the window again!"

And actually now, even now, after this terrible

quarter-hour of testing, Franz became aware that outside the window behind the Headmaster there was
pale green light, flecked with white and gold: out there
it must be warm, not hot, just pleasantly warm, the way
it always is in May, the best weather for playing
outdoors, for cops and robbers. Franz had learned how
to use clothesline poles to vault over the walls of back
yards—a sprint, pull yourself up and over. But in P.E.
he got a D, unsatisfactory. Just then he must have
made a movement that told the Headmaster he considered himself dismissed from the blackboard, from the
entire humiliating scrutiny of his ignorance of Greek.

"Stay where you are!" the Head ordered. "Perhaps
you would also be kind enough to place the accents on
the words! We don't do anything by halves here," he
informed Franz, "especially not in Greek. Greek
words without the accents that belong to them—that
would be. . . ." He broke off, powerless to convey
what an accentless Greek word meant to him, apparently something almost nauseating. Then he added:
"Perhaps you can improve the impression you have
made on me by showing that at least you have mas-
tered the accenting of Greek words."

That's all I need, thought Franz. The pale green
light vanished as he turned his back to the class again.
The board was black, a dirty black; once again he read
the sentence claiming that it was worthwhile to extol

the country. I don't know a thing about the accents, not a damn thing. On the off chance he placed an acute on the ε of ἐστιν. The Head said, "mhm," but as Franz was about to continue and tackle the αξια he stopped him with: "There is still something missing with *estin*."

What could still be missing there? pondered Franz, but a prolonged stare at the word brought no solution. Again the Head walked to the board and with his own hand placed another symbol in front of the acute, one that looked like a semicircle opening to the left. ἔστιν was now written on the board.

"Do you know at least what that symbol is called?" asked the Head, and on receiving no answer he continued: "*Spiritus lenis*. Smooth breathing. Since the Greeks had no letter for H, they expressed it by symbols. The odd thing is that they even had to use a symbol when they did not want an H in a word. Well now, let us proceed to *axia*."

Because the Head had stressed the second syllable, Franz quickly placed an acute on the ι. Now came *hēde* and *hē*, the goat-bleating; but before Franz could deal with the problem of putting accents on words that sounded as if an ancient Greek were leering over his shoulder, the Head restrained him again.

"So the word I have just pronounced for you is not *axia* but *haxia*," he said sarcastically.

"Oh, of course," said Franz and inserted the just-learned *spiritus lenis* over the α of the first syllable.

"Excellent," said the Head. He exhorted the class: "Let that be an example to you of a gift for rapid comprehension!" And when some of the boys tittered, he added: "I am quite serious. Kien has just proved that he can when he wants to."

But faced with the *hēde* and the *hē* Franz was stumped again. Dimly he was aware that it was not enough to put an acute accent over the *ē* of *hēde:* he had to come up with the aspirate, the symbol for the H that the ancient Greeks pronounced although it didn't exist in their alphabet. But he couldn't think of the symbol. Not for the life of me will I remember it because I never listen when that bore Kandlbinder holds forth. He talks, talks, talks, but he doesn't teach us anything.

"So there you stand, completely flummoxed," said the Head "because you don't know how the Greeks expressed H when they needed it to start a word. Yet you should know, for it was practically the first thing you were taught in your Greek lessons. But then, you don't find it necessary to pay attention, do you?" He gave a derogatory grunt, as if it were no longer worth taking trouble over Franz. But he was still holding the chalk and once again drew a semicircle above *ē*, only

this time the symbol opened toward the right.
"There," he said, "a bit of very obvious logical reflection should have led you to the conclusion that the
spiritus asper, the rough breathing, is simply the re-
verse of the *lenis*."

The phrase, "obvious logical reflection," made
Franz feel ashamed. He's right, he thought, it should
have occurred to me, but it often happens that I fail to
draw the most minor, the simplest conclusions; the
others are often much quicker at that. Hurriedly he
placed the *asper* on the solitary *hē* that followed the
hēde. The *khora* was easy: at last a word in this lousy
sentence that began with a consonant, so it was
enough to give the *o* an acute accent. "You were
lucky," commented the Head. "Strange that in *khora*
the Greeks used a short *omega*, so that here the acute
accent is actually enough." Now all that was left was
the *epaineisthai* the Head had corrected. No aspirate
preceded the first letter ε; consequently the *lenis* was
appropriate, and since the Head had stressed the third
syllable, the acute had to be placed above it, preferably above the ε of ει. Done!

But the Headmaster sadly shook his head.
"Epaineisthai," he said, unnaturally prolonging the *ei*
so that it sounded as if he were separating the vowels
"e" and "i." His voice rose to a shrill diphthong. "A
different sign for an accent is needed there!" he said.

"Make an effort, perhaps you will think of it!" With a
sigh he erased the acute over the ε and replaced it with
a horizontal wavy line over the ι.

"Do you at least know what this sign is called?" he
asked.

There's really no further point, thought Franz, in
my pretending that the answers to his questions just
happen to elude me for the moment. So he brought
out a "No," softly but without hesitation.

"It is called a circumflex," said the Head, nodding
as if he already knew that Franz would not even be
able to put a name to the sign. "The accents are to be
found on the third page of your grammar. You had
them weeks ago. It stands to reason anyway—no one
can advance as much as a single step in Greek until he
can recite the accents in his sleep.

"But you," he said, "you have missed it all. What
were you actually doing while the class was learning
about accents? Aletter!" he suddenly called out, turning toward the class. "Have a look under Kien's desk
and see if there isn't one of those trashy Karl May
books there!"

Hugo, the coward, is going to betray me, thought
Franz. Any moment now he's going to pull out *Through
Wildest Kurdistan* from the shelf under my desk. But
Hugo didn't betray him: he leaned across Franz's seat,
rummaged around for a while on his shelf, straight-

ened up, and said: "There are only a few exercise
books in there, Headmaster." Terrific, thought Franz,
Hugo is a decent fellow after all.

But again the Head's attention was diverted by the
sentence on the blackboard. He could not resist the
urge to read it out once more to Franz, from beginning
to end with the correct stress. So, with his emphases,
his falling and rising intonations, he recited it: "ἔστιν
ἀξία ἥδε ἡ χώρα ἐπαινεῖσθαι. Ah!" he exclaimed.
"That is the language of Homer and Sophocles! Do
you now grasp that Greek without its accents is unthinkable? They form the melody of this language,
turning even the simplest sentence into a work of
art—do you grasp that?"

"Yes," Franz replied meekly, for at that moment he
really had understood.

"Almost incredible," said the Head, resuming a
matter-of-fact, almost cynical tone, but it was also
clear from his voice that he felt flattered by the success
of his drill. And as if to reward the student for having
understood, he imparted something further from the
treasure chest of his knowledge by starting to write a
list on the empty space on the blackboard: oxytone,
Franz read, and underneath in a vertical column—
paroxytone, proparoxytone, perispomenon, properispomenon.

"Ever heard of these?" the Head asked. Without

waiting for a reply he went on: "Of course you have. I am sure your teacher has explained the terms that indicate the position of accents in a word. Only at that time, too, you were probably—well, let us say: daydreaming."

In his clearly legible, firm, and uncompromising hand he completed the chart. He even drew a box around it that he divided into three sections by two vertical lines. Franz read:

oxytone	acute, grave	final syllable
paroxytone	acute	penult
proparoxytone	acute	antepenult
perispomenon	circumflex	final syllable
properispomenon	circumflex	penult

"Copy that down, all of you!" the Head ordered the class. On hearing the rustle of exercise books he told Franz: "And you, Kien, explain to them the meaning of this chart."

With the hand holding the chalk he indicated the word "oxytone."

"An acute on the last syllable of a word is called an oxytone," said Franz, haltingly but at the same time thinking: It's easy as pie!

"Bravo," said the Head. "You're not stupid. Just lazy. *Quod erat demonstrandum.* Continue!"

Franz was about to define paroxytone, but he never got a chance, for at that moment Kandlbinder intervened. The expert in Dr. Kandlbinder could no longer bear listening in silence to the Head's teaching methods.

"But Headmaster," he began again, as before, although this time not indignant or offended but forcing himself to be mild and courteous as if wishing merely to reason with the Head: "But Headmaster, the ultimate, penultimate, and antepenultimate column applies not to accents but to whole words! It is not the accent that is called an oxytone but the whole word where an acute or grave appears over the last syllable."

The Head had listened speechlessly to this lecture. Then something happened that Franz, the entire class, and no doubt Kandlbinder too, would never have expected of him: he lost his temper.

"That's enough!" he hissed at the teacher. And again: "That's enough, Mr. Kandlbinder?"

He's even left out the "Doctor" this time, Franz noted: he's in such a rage that he addresses him simply as Mr. Kandlbinder. He's certainly letting him have it! And all because of me. What a heel I am not to care how the Head chews out Kandlbinder in front of the whole class.

"Here I pick one of the boys from your class," the Head carried on in his fury, "and what do I find? He has failed to grasp even the most simple basics of Greek. Ever since Easter, for the past six weeks, he has dared to idle away every lesson, and you"—his voice swelled to undisguised, angry thunder—"you have noticed absolutely nothing! Nothing, I say— don't deny it, otherwise you would have kept him in after school until he was blue in the face, or you would have come to me and said, frankly and honestly: There's nothing I can do with Kien. For what is so utterly scandalous about the Kien boy is not that he is indescribably lazy—lazybones of that caliber are to be found in every class—but that until this lesson he has managed to bluff his way all through your course. Tsk, tsk, tsk! And then you dare to interrupt me while I am putting him to the test, and at the very moment when I am dinning some rules of thumb into him that can help him catch up a bit, if he wants to. Although, of couse, it is too late because for six weeks you, Dr. Kandlbinder, have not been on the *qui vive*."

His use of the doctor title was a sign that he had himself under control again.

"Yes, dinning," he said, ending his attack on Kandlbinder and lapsing into a soliloquy. "At the *Gymnasium* in Freising they were quite merciless in dinning the oxytones and perispomena into us from the very beginning. And with no hair-splitting differentiation between words and accents. An accent on the last syllable, that was an oxytone, and a circumflex on the penult was a properispomenon—that's how we learned it at the Archepiscopal *Gymnasium* in Freising, and that was the right way, because it was simple. One has merely to hear a word like 'anthropos' to say to oneself, 'aha, proparoxytone,' and place the acute on the antepenult."

Aha my foot, thought Franz, I would do the same if the word was said out loud to me and I had never heard a thing about all this oxytone-and-so-on hogwash. Actually it's not simple, it's complicated if I first have to think "oxytone" before placing the acute. So he was waiting for Kandlbinder to contradict the Head but the teacher was shattered—not by the Head's highly disputable argument regarding the doctrine of emphasis but—this was obvious!—by the accusation of complete pedagogic failure in the case of his student Kien. To have been hauled over the coals in front of the entire Grade 8-B has robbed him of words. He knows that the affair will have a sequel in the Headmaster's study or at the faculty meeting. My God, thought Franz, I've really got him into a mess!

As if wanting to exonerate their teacher, at least partially, after all this, the Head once again pointed at the book lying on the desk. "The grammar you are using is not simple enough," he said. "If I cannot find a better one, I will write a simpler one for you myself."

Suddenly he pounced on Franz Kien again.

"Let's see if you can recite the accent rules!" he demanded. "But by heart! Without looking at the blackboard!"

"Oxytone," Franz began, slowly at first, then more and more fluently. "Paroxytone, proparoxytone, perispomenon, properispomenon." He was amazed at himself. How on earth did I manage that? he thought. Probably because this series of words pleases me. It is logical and sounds good.

"Well, there you are," said the Head, showing no surprise but visibly satisfied. His expression indicated that he had known what was coming, he was just acting the old schoolmaster again, thought Franz, the venerator of Socrates, the reader of Homer and Sophocles. He imagines he has proved that in five minutes he has taught me the Greek accent rules because I can instantly reel off his formula—it *is* melodious, a work of art, he's right about that, while Kandlbinder only drums signs into us. But if I were to take an interest in Greek I would rather study it according to the Kandlbinder method. By using my brain.

The Head had sufficient tact not to look triumphantly in Kandlbinder's direction. Instead he walked right up to Franz, even grasped the lapel of Franz's jacket with his right hand, and spoke to him in a voice so soft that it sounded like a whisper. But the whole

class can still hear what he's whispering, thought
Franz, it's all put on, his whispering, he can't possibly
speak so softly that they can't all hear it.

"Do you know what intelligent students do who
don't want to learn?" asked the Head. He acted as if
he were about to reveal a secret to Franz.

Franz was so dazed by the sudden closeness of the
Head, by this familiarity from a man who had wanted
all along to demolish him, simply demolish him, that
he wasn't even capable of assuming an expression of
polite inquiry in his eyes. He could feel only that he
was hanging by his jacket from the hand of this powerful man, and that he found this grip distasteful.

"They learn by heart," whispered the Head, as if
drawing Franz into a conspiracy. "If you had learned
by heart, at home, the sentence I have just drilled into
you, you would have deceived me brilliantly. Yes—
even me! I might never have realized that you have
not grasped it. And that would have cost you no more
than three minutes of your precious time. Three
minutes—and you could have rattled off the *estin axia*
as if there were nothing to it."

As swiftly as he had approached Franz, he moved
away from him. I don't like him, thought Franz, and
he's noticed it. I wish I knew why I don't like him. He
doesn't have B.O., or bad breath, he smells freshly
shaved. But it's his paunch I don't like, the paunch—

with the white shirt over it—that he's touched me
with.

And anyway, why did he throw himself at me? All of
a sudden he was no longer the stern examiner but
acted instead as if he wanted to give me a tip. But I
didn't fall for it, the way I did a few weeks ago in the
washroom. Now, since this time I didn't fall for it, he's
peeved.

The first and until now only time Franz had encoun-
tered the Head was in the students' washroom. Franz
had used the toilet during a break, and just as he was
stepping from the stall into the urinal area, the Head
had come in. That was odd: Franz had never seen a
teacher using a student can during a break—it must
have been a dire emergency for such a thing to happen. But the Head was in no hurry at all. Apparently
he merely wanted to inspect the toilets, just as he was
inspecting Grade 8-B today, and, just like today, he
had walked up to Franz. He had looked him up and
down with his kind blue, gold-rimmed eyes, so kind
that Franz not only greeted him respectfully, as the
rules required, but gave an expectant smile. I must
have been an idiot, thought Franz, to assume that in
such a place and because he was eyeing me so benevolently, the Head would say something amusing, but
he did, and that something amusing came from right
up close, in a matter-of-fact whisper, loud enough for

the other boys who happened to be at the urinals also to hear it clearly: "Your fly is still open, Kien. Arrange your clothing!"

And he knew my name, although I had never had anything to do with him. Like that. Just like that.

Today, however, the Head has not succeeded in making me blush beet-red, as he did the first time he came too close to me. Looking back, I can't reproach him for drawing my attention to the open fly, although it might have been better if a few minutes later Hugo or one of the others had grinned and made some vulgar remark. That would have been less embarrassing than the Head's look.

Today what I would have liked to tell him was: Remove your white paunch from my jacket! Would have, thought Franz. Unfortunately I'm not Konrad Greiff: he would have spat it out at him.

Yes, so now he's noticed that his coming-close, his washroom-whispering, his I-want-to-tell-you-a-secret, his crappy advice about learning by heart, hasn't accomplished a thing, not with me, that I don't accept his crappy advice because I don't want to be an intelligent student, I don't want to be a student at all. But what do I want to be? Christ almighty, I don't know— sometime later I'll know, later I'll know more than they can teach me here in their boring school, that stupid teacher and his overfed headmaster, I'll have no trouble teaching myself, baloney, who am I kidding, I'll be missing years if I don't get down to it and sweat, now, right now.

"You may go back to your seat," said the Head, but Franz knew immediately that he couldn't afford to feel relieved. To realize that the scene was not yet over didn't require Hugo Aletter to be sitting there with pursed lips, slowly shaking his head and muttering words of concern.

"You shouldn't have shown him so openly that you can't stand the sight of him," Hugo would be telling him a few days later, on one of Franz's last days at the Wittelsbach *Gymnasium*. But then Hugo was an ambitious student, and Franz would merely shrug off this wise utterance—how could he help it if he disliked old Himmler?

The latter had stepped down from the dais to the level of the class. For a while he paced up and down in front of the first row of desks, silently, his hands clasped behind his back. What a phony actor, thought Franz. Then he stopped, looked at the teacher, and asked: "What do you propose, Dr. Kandlbinder?"

At last Kandlbinder left his place by the door, came two steps closer, and said: "Tutoring."

The Head brought his arms from behind his back

and raised them in a final dismissive gesture. Then he said something that caused Franz's face to turn fiery red again.

"Tutoring is expensive," said the Head. "His father cannot afford it. Remember that he cannot even come up with the school fees. At his request we have waived Kien's school fees."

The bastard, thought Franz, the dirty bastard! To announce publicly that my father can't come up with the ninety marks a month for school fees! The hundred and eighty marks, because he can't afford to pay for Karl either, now that he's so ill and earning almost nothing. That filthy swine, thought Franz—it's really something, to stand there in front of the class trumpeting that we have been reduced to poverty, he's a filthy swine, this venerator of Socrates, a bastard, but who cares, let them all know that the Kiens are now poor, what do I care, thought Franz. His complexion returned to normal, although he was still thinking: the bastard! Not even what followed could rattle him; he listened calmly while the Head, still pretending to speak only to Kandlbinder, carried on:

"We have waived Kien's school fees at the request of his father although, according to regulations, we are not entitled to do so. School fees may be waived only for outstanding students. But I"—"I," he's saying now, thought Franz—"I believed that for the son of an officer who has been highly decorated for bravery and who, probably through no fault of his own, is experiencing financial hardship"—I like that "probably," thought Franz: my dad was only an officer in the Reserves, which is why he doesn't get a pension—"I believed," the Head continued, "that I could make an exception in the case of such a student. And how does he reward the school and his poor father?"

He collected himself before delivering the final blow, and Franz had now reached the point of being able to watch him without emotion.

"I even allowed him to be moved up into Grade 8," the Head went on. "With an F in math and a D in Latin. That was a serious mistake—I blame myself for it. After all, he had only made it into Grade 7 by the skin of his teeth. Year by year his performance in Latin has gone from bad to worse. And now it turns out that he intends to offer us the same spectacle in Greek—a student who imagines that he can simply exempt himself from studying the main subjects!"

He resumed his pacing to and fro between the cold, neutral wall in which the door was set and the window that was filled with the green light of May.

"No," he said to the silent Kandlbinder. "This won't do. This simply won't do. Tell me yourself: Are we to let him sit around here for the whole of the rest of the year until it is quite certain that in Greek, too, he will get an F, and only an F?"

He had not asked his question for the sake of getting a reply, and of course he received none. Kandlbinder maintained his silence, his head tilted to one side. Now the Head no longer needs to say he's going to write to my father, thought Franz, the way he's going to write to Greiff's father. It's already obvious that I'm being kicked out, that I have to go to school, to the Wittelsbach *Gymnasium,* for only a few more days. Oh boy, he suddenly thought, I don't have to walk that long, dreary route any more, from Neuhausen to Mars-Platz, along Juta- and Alphonse-Strasse, Nymphenburger-Strasse and Blutenburg-Strasse as far as the barracks and brewery district around Mars-Platz, the artillery barracks and the Hacker brewery, all those dreary streets I have to walk along every day—that's behind me now, I'm only sorry for Father, it'll be a terrible blow to him when he finds out.

The Head stopped. This time he looked not at Kandlbinder but at Franz.

"Your brother Karl is another one like you," he said. "How he managed to make it to Grade 10 is a mystery to me. I have had a look at his most recent assignment sheets. Full of mistakes! But in a neat handwriting—he will never graduate with that. I will see to that."

I can't believe it, thought Franz—to kick Karl out of school too! Two sons at the same time! It'll be the end of Father. It's what's been keeping him going—the hope that we would go on to university.

Unexpectedly the Head abandoned his official, menacing tone. "Tell me, how is your father?" he asked. Franz was floored. That really takes the cake, he thought: first to throw Karl and me out of school while at the same time humiliating Father in front of the entire class because of the school fees, and then to inquire after his health! The lousy hypocrite!

"He's sick," Franz replied sullenly. "Very sick. Has been for a long time."

"Oh," said the Head, "I'm sorry to hear that. So he won't be pleased to learn that his sons are not fit for a high-school education."

So again nothing but a put-down! A word or two of regret, but only to show that the father's illness would do nothing to alter the fate of the sons.

Strangely enough, Father didn't take the bad news as much to heart as Franz had feared. He did not fly into a rage as he normally did when Franz came home with his miserable report cards. Franz had made up his mind to be the one to tell him that he was going to be thrown out of school; he didn't want his father to hear of it first from the Headmaster's letter. Perhaps Father remained so calm because he had already lain down on the sofa, after supper. At that time he'd just begun giving himself morphine injections, with the permission of the doctors at the Schwabing Hospital, because of the pain in his right foot, the gangrene in his toes, which were soon to be amputated. The big toe of his right foot had already turned black. His father, looking very pale, lay on the sofa; he had long ceased to be a hot-tempered man with a face that tended to turn crimson under black hair.

The sofa stood with its head toward the window, beyond which night had already fallen. A lamp with a green silk shade shone down on the cleared dining-table. Franz's mother had placed a smooth board on the table and was kneading dough that she took from a large earthenware jar. Franz watched her; he liked to watch his mother kneading dough to make noodles. Without a word, his brother Karl had listened until Franz had finished his story from school, which obviously concerned him too. Then he sat down at the piano and, as he had been doing every evening in recent weeks, picked out the notes of a Schubert Impromptu without quite getting it right. Still, to Franz the music sounded beautiful. At a pause in the music, Father said: "His inquiry after my health—that was only because I have the Iron Cross First Class."

Could be, thought Franz. The pencil-pushers at the base were secretly scared of the front-line soldiers; somehow they feared the front-liners would one day settle accounts with them, which was why they pretended to be their buddies and asked after their health. Yes, there was some truth in it; on the other hand, envy was involved as well. No doubt the Head, too, was envious of Father's Iron Cross First Class. And Franz couldn't believe his ears as he listened to what came next.

"Besides," Father went on, "old Himmler wants to get on the right side of me because he knows his son is one of my comrades in the Reich Banner."

But Father's all wrong there, thought Franz. If the Head really believes that my dad is on friendly terms with his son, young Himmler, that would be the very reason to dislike him.

His mother joined in. After rolling out the dough very thin she began cutting it into strips with a sharp knife.

"Isn't there a Mrs. Himmler, then?" she asked. "It seems to me that, if there is, it would be up to her to see that her husband and son get along with each other."

Franz Kien senior made no reply. He had closed his eyes—whether because of the pain or because he had fallen asleep, Franz couldn't tell. Maybe Father was merely feigning drowsiness because he didn't want to reply.

Franz answered his mother himself.

"Old Himmler wears a wide gold wedding-band," he told her, wondering at the same time whether the Head's wedding-band was also merely a part of the mask the great schoolmaster had assumed and wore all his life.

Too bad his father was already asleep. He would also have liked to tell him how he had felt that morning at the shrill sound of the bell in the corridor. The Head had left the room immediately, not wanting to be caught in the ruthless stampede of the eighth graders. He had nodded briefly to the students and to Kandlbinder, and once again the classroom door had opened to him without his having to touch it. Like all the others, Franz had gathered up his books and papers and stuffed them into his worn leather satchel. The others were shouting all around him, but no one said a word to Franz, although they didn't seem unfriendly. They seemed to look away when their eyes happened to meet his. Did Konrad Greiff exchange a glance with him? Franz couldn't have said for sure; only Mr. Kandlbinder looked at him steadily and reproachfully as long as he was in the room. Franz hurried to get away. Outside it was warm; sunlight shone on the dreary streets. On the way home, none of his classmates joined him, but that afternoon passed like every other afternoon: he played soccer on the Lacherschmied field, and among the other boys there wasn't one who went to the Wittelsbach *Gymnasium*. Franz played poorly; he had a sinking feeling as he thought of the talk he would have to have that evening with his father.

Instead of the shrill ringing of the school bell, he now heard only his brother's tinkling at the piano, and soon that broke off. Franz's little brother—eight years younger than Franz—was already asleep in the bed that stood across from his own. For a while, using his flashlight, Franz read *Through Wildest Kurdistan*, his head propped on his right arm. Then he switched off the light and lay back on his pillow.

Perispomenon, he thought, properispomenon, before he fell asleep.

AFTERWORD

— 1 —

In writing five stories (the present one being the sixth) that describe certain circumstances in my life, I invented a person by the name of Franz Kien who experiences these events. Why did I do this? Haven't I more than once unequivocally declared that these Franz Kien stories deal with memories of myself, that they are attempts at an autobiography in story-form? Franz Kien is myself. But if that is the case, why do I bring him in at all instead of simple saying "I"? Why do I write about myself in the third person rather than the first? It was *I*, after all, I and no one else who was tested in Greek by the elder Mr. Himmler and, due to the deplorable results, was expelled from that classical *Gymnasium*. Why the devil do I hold a mask—this Kien, a name, a mere name—up to my face?

I have no answer to this. Since I am as allergic to subtleties as the schoolboy Franz Kien (my other self) was to his Headmaster's stale tirades about Socrates and Sophocles, I firmly reject the excuse that Franz Kien owes his existence to my wish to preserve a certain discretion. The intensely personal—the author might imagine—loses something of the embarrassing nature of a confession when attributed to a third person, no matter how threadbare that person's disguise may be. But in fact the exact opposite is the case, for a narrative mode in the third person is the very form that allows the author the utmost degree of honesty. It enables him to overcome inhibitions that it is scarcely possible to shed when he says "I." In short: it is a trifle easier to record that some "he" or other—for example, Franz Kien in *Old Periphery*—has broken a promise to his friends than to write the blunt confession: I let down my friends.

That, anyway, is what the author is tempted to believe. The desire to be discreet is, after all, one of his more laudable attributes. Most of his readers share this desire, having had enough of authors who crudely blurt out their life stories. But autobiography requires that an author not be dishonest about himself; it is not a game of hide-and-seek. Moreover, it would be of no advantage to me: no one will take Franz Kien for Franz Kien. A whim, the reader will say in either annoyance or sympathy—a whim that does not justify the author's choice not to speak about himself.

I find this choice seems even more mysterious when I remind myself that for other autobiographical pieces

I have not hesitated to use the narrative mode of first person singular. *The Cherries of Freedom* and *The Dufflebag* are memoirs; on the other hand I have also written a novel, *Efraim's Book,* in the I-mode, yet, unlike Franz Kien, Efraim is in no way identical with myself but an entirely different person: I must insist on that. Incidentally, that novel concludes with the thought that of all masks the "I" may be the best. Such are the contradictions that haunt a writer's workshop.

I suspect, however—and this is the only hypothesis I permit myself concerning the existence of Franz Kien—that the intention of recalling my life in stories has played a trick on me. It is the very form that, if not exactly compelling me to make use of Franz Kien, does advise me to do so. Kien allows me a certain narrative freedom not permitted by "I"—that tyrannical form of verb conjugation. "I see" does not allow one to see anything other than what "I" see, saw, or will see, whereas "he" is not bound to such a rigorous limitation of his field of vision. I am referring not to what goes on in Kien's mind, or to the part played by imagination in the text, which must not deviate by a hair's breadth from what goes on in my own mind, my own imagination! I speak only of the furnishings I place on the stage of my memory, the stage on which I cause him to act. To give an example: The Konrad von Greiff episode in *The Father of a Murderer* took place not during the Greek lesson described in this story but on some other occasion. (There has never been any lack of opportunity in the drama of the authoritarian German school to interpolate scenes of adaptation.) By laying this card on the table, do I render my story implausible, false according to the rules of autobiography? I think not. On the contrary, my action seems to me to have rendered it more authentic. In any case, autobiography need "only" be authentic. Within the limitations imposed by this demand, it may do whatever it pleases.

My point is that, had I laid claim to personal experience of the case of the haughty aristocratic student in that class, I would have—well, not exactly lied, but I would have been telling a fib. Whereas I could not permit myself even that harmless a pleasure, it is permissible for Kien to have observed the incident. In his story, the Wittelsbach *Gymnasium* in the year 1928 becomes more clearly illuminated than in the strict "I" of absolute autobiography. The narrative form sustains a tension with the spirit of autobiography. Something remains unresolved in such texts—I admit this. In fact, that is my intention.

So much, at least, for Franz Kien. He is an intractable fellow.

—— 2 ——

My school reports are the only personal documents
from my childhood and youth that survived the second
World War. The Headmaster of the Wittelsbach *Gymnasium* signed them: Himmler. No first name, and I
must not invent one for him. There is only one item
about him that I have invented: his claim to have attended the Archepiscopal *Gymnasium* in Freising. For
me there is no queston but that such a man as Himmler senior was educated at a cadre school of Bavarian
ultramontanism; he might equally well have been a
pupil at Ettal, Andechs, or Regensburg—it is not that
important. On the other hand, I have had to refrain
from citing other, indisputable facts known to me
about him: for instance, the fact that later, when his
son had become the second-most powerful man in the
German Reich, the elder Himmler became reconciled
with his son. An S.S. guard of honor fired a salute over
his coffin. But maybe that happened against his
wishes? Maybe the elder Himmler continued to curse
his son from his deathbed? Such supplementary de-
tails are not so certain after all. Franz cannot supply
them because he knows no more about the Head than
what his father told him and what he saw and heard in
that Greek lesson as well as at their brief encounter in
the students' washroom. A glance into the future, ob-

tainable by a simple technique known as a flash-
forward, would completely destroy the character of the
story as a strictly autobiographical reminiscence. In
such an account, the Head and Kien (my other self)
must amount to no more than they did on a certain day
in May 1928. Only in this way do they, and with them
the story, remain open. Their narrator, on that certain
day in May 1928, had no idea what was in store for
him, much less for the elder Himmler, and he hopes
that his readers will also prefer an open story to a
closed one. One should not be able to file stories away
like a sales agreement or a will.

Only the title projects the story into a future,
encapsulating as it does the irrefutable truth that
Himmler senior was the father of a murderer. The
term "murderer" for Heinrich Himmler is a mild one.
He was not just any perpetrator of a capital crime but,
as far as my knowledge of history goes, the greatest
destroyer of human life who ever existed. However,
my chosen title merely embraces a historical fact; it
makes no claim to determine the private, personal
truth of this man, the Head. Was the elder Himmler
predestined to become the father of the younger? Was
it a matter of "natural inevitability"—i.e., in line with
plausible psychological principles, with the laws that
govern the struggle between one generation and the
next and the paradoxical consequences of family

tradition—that such a father must produce a son? Were they both, father and son, the products of an environment and a political situation, or were they victims of Fate, which we Germans like to regard as inescapable?

I admit to having no answer to these questions, and I will go even farther and declare categorically that I would never have told this story from my youth if I knew with certainty that the monster and the schoolmaster are interdependent, and how. Or whether neither determines the other at all. In that case they would not have interested me. An interest that causes me to sit down with a pencil before a stack of blank paper is aroused solely by the perception of open character, not of people about whom I know every last detail before I begin to write. And the people I like best are those who remain open, mysterious, even after I have finished writing.

That is all I have to say about the content of my account. My only reason for offering this fragment of a commentary is to eliminate the crudest misinterpretation: No one should imagine that, with *The Father of a Murderer*, I am casting aspersions on the Himmler clan, even though Franz Kien does this to a degree by showing some understanding for the son—whom he does not know—as against the father, whom he profoundly dislikes.

Let me merely note that it is worth reflecting that Heinrich Himmler—and for this my memory supplies the proof—did not grow up in the dregs of society, as did the man to whose hypnosis he succumbed, but in a family of the old-established, classically educated bourgeoisie. Does this mean that humanism offers no protection whatsoever? The question may well plunge one into despair.

I escaped this despair by trying to write the story of a boy who does not want to learn. And not even in this respect is the story unequivocal: there will be readers who, faced with the confrontation between the Head and Franz Kien, take the side of the Headmaster. Personally, though—this much I must be granted—I take my own side.

It might seem that the direct speech in which the dialogues are reproduced contradicts the autobiographical and hence quasi-documentary truth claimed for the story. Any even mildly critical reader will object that it is impossible to recall a dialogue verbatim after more than fifty years. I can only ask those readers to reflect once again on the function of the figure of Franz Kien, on the possibility accorded me by resorting to that figure of the third person and thus avoiding the cumbersome subjective construction, required in German by indirect speech, that so easily slows down the tempo even when the text does not call for it.

The narrative method used for *The Father of a Murderer* is simplicity itself: strictly linear. The story covers the events that took place from the first minute to the last of a class period. Apart from that, the text limits itself to a single flash-back (an account of what Franz Kien's father told his son about the Head), and a single flash-forward (the family scene at the end). Limiting the narrative to the unity of time and space resulted, almost automatically, in that literary form known as the extended short story.

One problem I failed to solve was that of narrative levels, of which there are three in this story. The first is that of the author, i.e., my own, in such simple sentences as "Franz Kien thought." Even so small a fraction of a sentence as this presupposes someone who knows what Franz Kien was thinking. The second and most extensive level belongs to Kien himself; he is the protagonist not only of the action but also of the reflections on that action. And finally there is a third party registering the incident: a collective one, the class. I did not succeed in fitting these narrative fields one over the other to make them coincide, and I tend to think that such an attempt can never succeed, unless entirely different reproduction techniques are employed.

So why didn't you make use of them, I will be asked? Why indeed? Because the linear method, in spite of its inadequacies, seemed to me in this case to be the right one. Classroom with teachers: I was fascinated by the idea of digging out that snapshot.

No individual narrative level was to be accorded the Headmaster and Kandlbinder. They were no more than objects of pure observation, which gives them the slight advantage that some readers may consider them to be the victims of gross injustice. I do not share this view, although I admit that, even after more than fifty years, I am still prejudiced in my judgment. The recording of memories is always subjective. But that does not mean it is untrue.

Accurately reproducing the thought and language of Kien and his classmates turned out to be my most difficult task, requiring me to use the vocabulary and idioms of Bavarian schoolboys in the late 1920s and make them sound convincing rather than like extraneous highlights. Since I was born and raised in Munich and consequently speak the Bavarian dialect, one solution might have been to compose a work of true dialect literature, but that didn't appeal to me. I realized I must renounce the entire inventory of modern slang, and this was difficult; for since the admirable vocabulary of 1970s slang did not exist in the 1920s, I had to make do without it. I was therefore limited to the vocabulary of my youth, of which, incidentally, some specimens have found their way from the level of jargon to a more durable status. So I have tried to color my story with the vernacular of its setting, and as unobtrusively as possible; a few light touches are enough. Language, I am convinced, always renews itself from the vernacular. Living literature seeks its delicate path between classicism and vulgarity—demands that I make of myself. Have I succeeded in fulfilling them? I don't know. I really don't. At least my readers should know what I am trying to accomplish.

*

I wish to thank Dr. Gertrud Marxer, of Kilchberg, Switzerland, for her kind assistance in reconstructing the Greek lesson described in the story.

*

Begun May 1979. Completed January 1980, Berzone (Valle Onsernone). A.A.